This edition produced for The Book People Ltd, Hall Wood Avenue,
Haydock, St Helens, WA11 9UL

First published in hardback in Great Britain by HarperCollins Publishers Ltd in 1996
First published in Picture Lions in 1999
3 5 7 9 10 8 6 4
ISBN: 0 00 762735 1

Picture Lions is an imprint of the Children's Division, part of HarperCollins Publishers Ltd

The HarperCollins website address is www.fireandwater.com

Manufactured in China

THE BADGER'S
BATH

NICK BUTTERWORTH

TED SMART

The badger had been doing what badgers do best. Digging. He'd had a lovely day and, as usual when he'd had a lovely day, he was filthy dirty.

"I'm very sorry," said Percy the park keeper, "but you can't come to tea like that."

The badger looked disappointed.

"You'll just have to have a bath," said Percy.

The badger looked even more disappointed.

First, Percy filled a tin bath with warm soapy water. Then he brought out all the things that he liked to use himself when he had a bath. Soap, a loofah, his backbrush, a sponge, some shampoo and, of course, his rubber duck.

The badger sniffed at the soapy water. He didn't like it. He didn't like it at all.

Percy thought for a moment. Then he disappeared and came back with a jug which he used for wetting his hair and a shower cap which he used for not wetting it.

"There. I think that's everything," said Percy. He turned to the badger. "Now, all we need . . ." But the badger was nowhere to be seen.

"Hmm . . ." said Percy. "Now all we need is the badger."

The badger was hiding. He didn't want a bath.

Percy searched and searched but he couldn't find the badger anywhere. He was getting very hot and bothered.

"I really can't understand it," he said. "I always enjoy a bath myself."

Percy sighed as he looked at the bath full of soapy water. Then he had an idea. He went into his hut.

W hen Percy came out again he was wearing his swimming trunks.

"Well, why not?" he said to himself. He chuckled as he stepped out of his boots and into the bath.

Percy lay back in the warm water and gazed up through the overhanging branches of a tree.

"Silly old badger," thought Percy. "I wonder where he's hiding."

There was a sudden rustling above his head and something black and white moved amongst the leaves. A strange idea came into Percy's mind.

"No... surely not?" he said to himself. "Badgers don't climb trees. It must have been a magpie."

The rustling noise came again.

Suddenly, there was a loud CRACK! With a great howl, a large black and white animal fell out of the tree, straight into Percy's bath water. SP-LOOSH!

For a moment, the badger completely disappeared. Then his head popped up through the soap suds, coughing and spluttering.

P ercy was spluttering too, but with
laughter.

"I see you changed your mind about
having a bath," he chuckled. "I suppose
you didn't want to miss your tea!"

"I didn't know badgers climbed trees," said Percy.

"Well," said the badger, "we're better at digging." He sighed. "Could you pass me the loofah, please?"

NICK BUTTERWORTH was born in North London
in 1946 and grew up in a sweet shop in Essex. He now lives
in Suffolk with his wife Annette and their two children,
Ben and Amanda.

The inspiration for the Percy the Park Keeper books
came from Nick Butterworth's many walks through the
local park with the family dog, Jake. The stories have sold
over two million copies and are loved by children all
around the world. Their popularity has led to the making
of a stunning animated television series, now available on
video from HIT Entertainment plc.

Read all the stories about Percy and his animal friends. . .

then enjoy the Percy activity books.

And don't forget you can now see Percy on video too!